Bears Make the Best

READING BUDDIES

written by Carmen Oliver
illustrated by Jean Claude

Curious Fox CF

a Capstone company—publishers for children

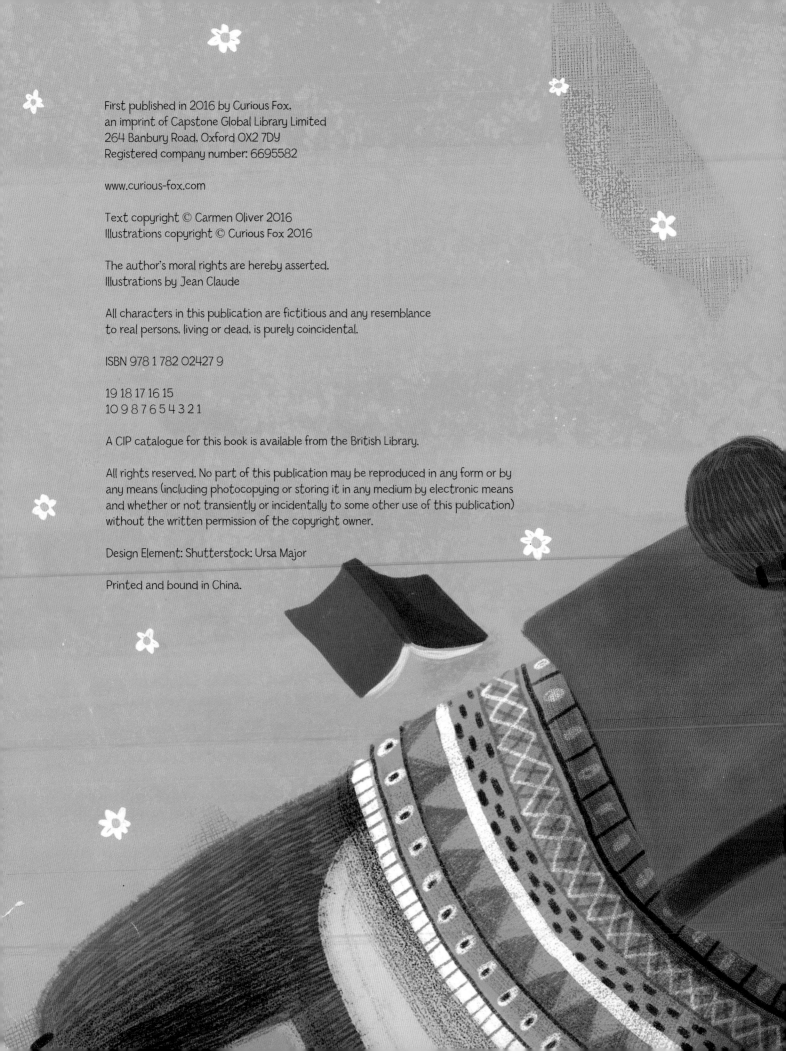

First published in 2016 by Curious Fox,
an imprint of Capstone Global Library Limited
264 Banbury Road, Oxford OX2 7DY
Registered company number: 6695582

www.curious-fox.com

ISBN 978 1 782 02427 9

19 18 17 16 15
10 9 8 7 6 5 4 3 2 1

A CIP catalogue for this book is available from the British Library.

Design Element: Shutterstock: Ursa Major

Printed and bound in China.

For Caldwell Heights Elementary, continue to read and soar!
And for Cassidy, Halle and Wyatt - the best
reading buddies a mom could ask for!
- Carmen

To Skye, Calum, Sam and Fin - keep reading, buddies!
- J.C.

At the beginning of the school year,
Mrs. Fitz-Pea assigned reading buddies,
but Adelaide didn't need one.
She already had her own!

"Don't be scared,"
Adelaide coaxed.
"Come in."

AHHHHHH!

"Wait!" Adelaide said.
"Bears make the best
reading buddies
and I'll tell you why."

"Bears know how to sniff out a good book with their super-powered snouts.

They're wild about adventures . . .

and mysteries . . .

and fairy tales."

"They know how to build peaceful places where no one bothers you while you read.

They sit side by side,
knee to knee, and put
the book between you,
so you both can see."

"Bears listen with their super-sensitive ears while you sound out the words.

And if you get frustrated, they wrap you up in warm bear hugs."

"Oh! And their claws are
perfect page-flipping tools . . .

...most of the time."

Rrriiip!

"But don't worry! They always carry a spare jar of honey for making repairs."

"Bears know you never run away from hard-to-pronounce words. They challenge you to look at the pictures and chew over the possibilities.

Quick Object Yellow How Antarctic Anemone Thermometer Rabbit Perplex Quan lonely farthe

And when you get it right . . ."

"... they stand on their hind legs
and roar so you'll keep going."

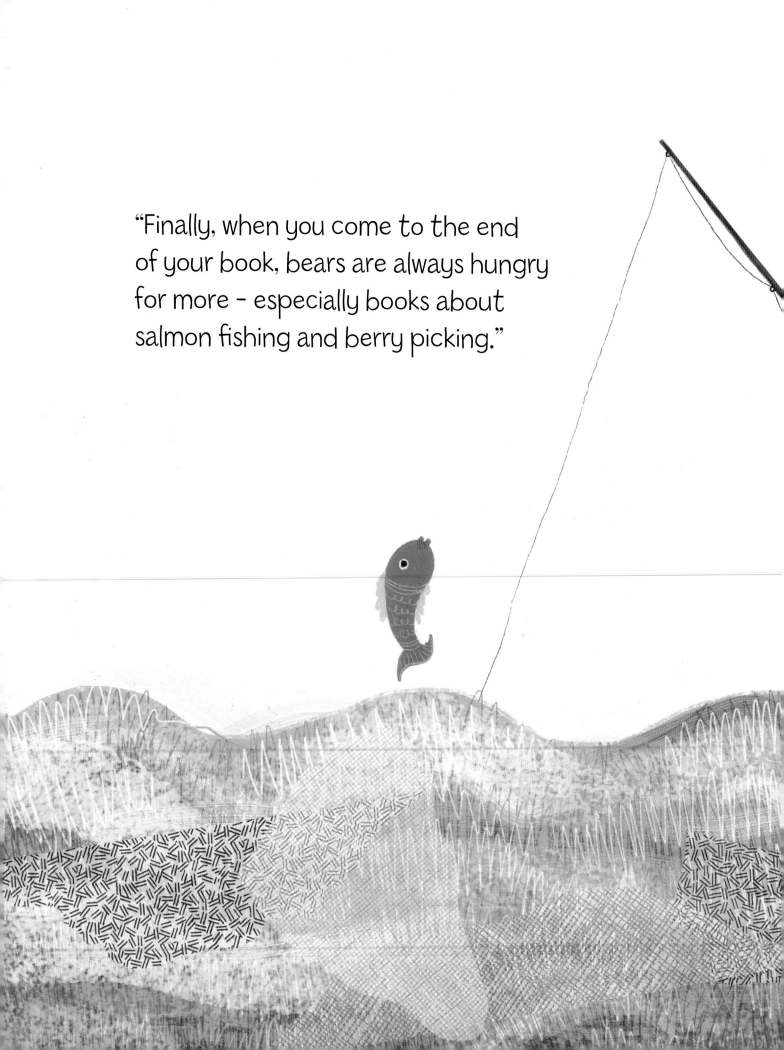

"Finally, when you come to the end of your book, bears are always hungry for more – especially books about salmon fishing and berry picking."

"Bears know that once you get a taste for books, you'll discover trail after trail of adventure and clamber to new heights."

"And that is why bears make the very best reading buddies," Adelaide finished.

"Well, don't just stand there, Adelaide," said Mrs. Fitz-Pea. "Show that bear in!"

"I'll read to you," Adelaide said.
"Then you can read to me."

And when Adelaide started to read,
Bear burrowed in and got lost in the story.